Around the World in Eighty Days

Jules Verne
Adapted by Jane Bingham

Illustrated by Adam Stower

Reading Consultant: Alison Kelly
University of Surrey Roehampton

Contents

Chapter 1

The journey begins

Over one hundred years ago, there
lived a man named Phileas Fogg.
For many years, he led a very quiet
life. He spent every day at his club,
which was where rich men went to
meet their friends.

Every morning, he left his house at exactly 11:30 and walked 576 steps to his club.

Then he ate lunch.

After lunch, Fogg read three newspapers from cover to cover. Then he ate supper. After that, he played cards with friends.

On the stroke of midnight, he went home to bed... before doing exactly the same the next day.

But one Wednesday everything changed. Fogg read some amazing news in his paper.

"Listen to this," he announced to his friends. "It says it's possible to travel around the world in only eighty days!"

I don't believe it!

You'd jump from train to ship to train again non-stop.

Despite his friends' laughter, Fogg was convinced he could do it.

When one friend bet that it couldn't be done, Fogg replied, "I will bet twenty thousand pounds that I can go around the world in eighty days or less!"

Everyone thought he was crazy but Fogg had made up his mind.

"I shall be back on December 21st," he said.

See you in eighty days!

As soon as he arrived home, Fogg asked Passepartout, his butler, to pack a small bag. Luckily, Passepartout had been an acrobat and could move quickly.

We're leaving on a round-the-world trip. Tonight!

In less than ten minutes, they were on their way to the station...

and at 8:45 exactly, the train pulled out. Fogg and Passepartout were off on their great adventure.

They were heading for the coast, where they could catch a boat to France. But they were also heading straight for trouble.

Chapter 2

Arriving in Africa

Dangerous thief

Wanted
dead or alive!

While Phileas Fogg was crossing Europe, the police were hunting a runaway thief. Only a few days before, he had stolen the huge sum of fifty-five thousand pounds from the Bank of England.

An inspector named Fix was convinced the thief would escape by sailing from Europe to Africa. He was waiting on the quay when Fogg reached Suez in North Africa.

Fogg sent Passepartout to get his passport stamped. "I need proof of the trip," he explained.

Quite by chance, Passepartout happened to ask Inspector Fix the way to the passport office.

When Fix saw the passport, he gasped. Fogg's description exactly matched the description of the thief. Fix was certain he'd found his man.

But he couldn't act at once. First, he needed some papers, which would allow him to arrest the thief.

So, Fix found out where Fogg was going and sent an urgent message to London. "Am on the trail of the thief. Following him to India. Send arrest papers to Bombay."

Fix quickly packed a small bag and boarded the ship for India.

The voyage was rough, but Fogg stayed as calm as ever. He ate four meals a day and played cards. He might have been at home.

Two days early, the ship steamed into Bombay. Inspector Fix was ready to make his arrest, but the papers had not arrived.

"My only hope," Fix decided, "is to stop Fogg from leaving India." Later that day, he saw his chance.

Passepartout had visited a temple but he didn't realize he was supposed to take off his shoes. When a priest tugged them from his feet, he started a fight.

Fix was delighted. "Now I've seen that butler break the law, I can make sure he's arrested and jailed here – along with his master!"

Fix followed Passepartout to the station and watched him catch a train. "See you in Calcutta," Fix muttered to himself. "I'll get your Mr. Fogg there."

Chapter 3

Fogg to the rescue

The train puffed its way through India, passing magnificent temples and fields of coffee and cotton. Passepartout saw it all, amazed. Fogg found a man to play cards.

But halfway through the third day, the train came to a stop.

"The track ends here," a guard announced. "It starts again in fifty miles at Allahabad."

Passepartout was furious. "How will we reach Calcutta in time?" he demanded.

Fogg didn't seem worried. "I've allowed time for delays," he said quietly. "We simply need to find another way to travel."

Passepartout rushed off. Soon, he was back with the answer.

Look! An elephant!

The elephant was expensive but Fogg didn't mind. He invited his card-playing friend to join them.

Then he hired a guide and, half an hour later, they were lurching through the jungle. Passepartout bounced up and down with glee. Every now and then, he tossed the elephant a sugar lump.

They journeyed for hours, crossing forests of date trees and sandy plains. That night, they camped in a ruined bungalow.

They were off again at six the next morning, breakfasting on bananas picked from a tree.

They had almost crossed a thick forest, when they heard music and voices. A large procession was snaking its way through the trees.

In the middle of the procession, a group of warriors carried the body of a dead prince. Behind them, two priests were pulling a beautiful girl.

Passepartout was shocked. "What are they doing?" he cried.

"It's the custom," their guide explained. "When a prince dies, his wife must die too, so they can go to heaven together."

"Tomorrow, Princess Aouda will be burned to death beside her husband."

Passepartout was horrified. Even Phileas Fogg, who let nothing disturb him, seemed upset.

"I have twelve hours to spare," he observed. "Let's save her."

By nightfall, the procession had reached a small temple. The princess was locked firmly inside. Everything seemed hopeless, until Passepartout had an idea...

I think I can see how to rescue her.

Next morning, Princess Aouda
was laid beside her husband. Then
the priests lit a huge fire, watched
by a silent crowd. Suddenly, the air
filled with screams. Some people
even flung themselves to the ground.
The dead prince was sitting up.

His ghostly figure rose through the smoke and grasped Princess Aouda in his arms. Then he strode off into the jungle.

"Let's go!" the ghost called to Fogg. It was Passepartout, who had disguised himself as the prince. Fogg and his friend chased after them, dodging bullets and arrows as they ran to safety.

Chapter 4

Tricked!

At Allahabad, Fogg gave the
elephant to their guide and jumped
on a train. But Fix had reported
Passepartout's fight at the temple.
As they arrived in Calcutta, Fogg
and Passepartout were grabbed by
police and taken to court.

Fogg and Passepartout faced a week in jail. The poor butler felt terrible. Then Fogg offered the court two thousand pounds.

"Very well," said the judge. "You may go free for now. But we'll keep the money if you don't return."

Aha... He's spending all the stolen money!

Fogg caught his next ship, to Hong Kong, with an hour to spare.

Fix was furious. "But Hong Kong belongs to Britain," he thought. "I can arrest Fogg there."

Princess Aouda, who hoped to find her cousin in Hong Kong, went too. When the ship stopped for coal in Singapore, Fogg and the princess went for a carriage ride.

They drove past pepper plants and nutmeg trees, grinning monkeys and grimacing tigers.

Near the end of the voyage, the ship battled against a raging wind. Fogg remained perfectly calm, but Passepartout was in a panic. "We'll miss our next ship, I know it!"

In the end, they reached Hong Kong one day late. Fogg had missed his next ship, which was to Yokohama in Japan.

"I knew it!" cried Passepartout.

Fix was delighted. "Now Fogg's stuck here and I can arrest him!" But luck was not on Fix's side.

It turned out that the ship to Yokohama had also been delayed, so Fogg hadn't missed it at all. Even worse, Fix's arrest papers still hadn't arrived.

Fix was desperate. Somehow, he had to keep Fogg in Hong Kong until the papers came.

Fogg booked a hotel for that night and set off to find Aouda's cousin. He sent Passepartout to reserve three cabins on their ship.

On the quay, Passepartout heard that the ship was sailing that very evening – and so did Fix.

"I must find my master!" the butler cried. But Fix invited him to a smoky inn for a drink first.

"I'm a detective and your master is a thief!" declared Fix, at the inn.

"Nonsense!" said Passepartout.

"Fogg mustn't know his ship sails tonight," thought Fix and bought the butler several drinks.

Before long, Passepartout was snoring and Fix had slipped away.

Fogg was on the quay early next morning and Princess Aouda was still with him. Her cousin had already left Hong Kong – and so, of course, had their ship. There was no sign of Passepartout either.

I'm afraid the ship left last night. I missed it too!

The next steamer wasn't leaving for a week. But Fogg did not give up easily. Instead, he looked for another boat to take him to Japan.

Finally, Fogg found a captain of a small boat who agreed to take them to Shanghai. "You can catch another steamer for Yokohama from there," he said. Seeing Fix on the quay, Fogg offered him a lift.

Before the boat left, Fogg searched all over Hong Kong for Passepartout. But his butler had vanished.

For two days, the little boat sped through the waves. Then a great storm blew up and gigantic waves crashed upon the deck. The boat was tossed around on the sea like a ball.

When at last the wind dropped, they had lost precious time. Even with all the sails hoisted, the boat couldn't go fast enough.

Then Fogg spotted a steamer.

"That's the one from Shanghai to Yokohama," said the captain.

"Signal her," said Fogg.

With a bang, a rocket soared into the air and the ship steamed over. As soon as it reached them, Fogg, Aouda and Fix clambered aboard.

But, in the meantime, what had
happened to Passepartout?

He had woken up just in time
to catch the ship to Japan. Rushing
on board at the last minute, he
discovered – to his horror – that
Fogg wasn't there.

When they landed at Yokohama, Passepartout didn't know what to do. He was wandering around in despair, when he saw a poster.

"Maybe I could join the acrobats!" he said to himself. "They're going to America and that's where Fogg is heading next."

"Can you sing, standing on your head, with a top on your left foot and a sword on your right?" asked the owner of the group. Passepartout nodded. "You're in!"

That evening, he took part in his first show, at the bottom of a human triangle. The crowd loved it. But suddenly...

all

the

acrobats

collapsed

in

a

heap.

Passepartout had spotted Phileas
Fogg, jumped up and run over.

Chapter 5

Racing home

They had no time for explanations. Fogg and his beaming butler raced to catch their next ship, for San Francisco. Princess Aouda, who had nowhere else to go, came too. She grew fonder of Fogg each day.

As the ship steamed on, Passepartout began to think Fogg would win his bet. But one day he saw Fix on deck. The inspector had secretly followed them.

I'm sorry I tricked you.

Passepartout hit him.

"Wait!" cried Fix. "It might have seemed I was against you before—"

"You were!" said Passepartout.

"Well, yes," agreed Fix, "and I still think Fogg's a thief. But now I want him in England. It's only in England I can arrest him."

Passepartout didn't want to worry Fogg, so he kept quiet about Fix. But when Fogg went to get his passport stamped in San Francisco, he bumped into the inspector too.

"What a surprise!" lied Fix and joined them on the next stage of the journey, crossing America by train.

The Pacific Railroad steamed right across the country to New York. It had every luxury on board, from shops to restaurants, but it still had to wait when a herd of buffalo crossed the track.

The next obstacle was a shaky
bridge. "I'll cross at top speed!"
said the driver. He went so fast the
wheels barely touched the tracks.

The train reared up and jumped
across. As it landed on the other
side, the bridge crashed into
the river.

Soon after that, they hit real trouble. The train was steaming by some rocky cliffs, when a band of Sioux warriors jumped onto its roof. The warriors quickly took over driving the train.

There's a fort by the next station, but they'll never let the train stop there.

Don't worry. I'll stop it!

Passepartout sped into action.

Crawling under the train, he wriggled and swung all the way to the engine, without being seen.

Then he unhooked the engine and the train slowly came to a halt... just beside the station.

But when Fogg looked for his butler a few seconds later, he'd gone.

"The warriors took him when they fled!" shouted a guard.

Calling over some soldiers, Fogg went into the hills to look for him.

It took all day to find and free Passepartout. They had to camp out overnight and only got back to the station the following morning.

By then, their train had long since left and the next one wasn't due until that evening.

"I've done it again," wailed the butler. But Fix came to the rescue.

"I've just met a man who owns a land yacht," he announced.

Soon, they were gliding over the snow. Wind filled the yacht's sails and it whizzed over the icy plains.

They caught up with the train for New York at the very next station. It puffed across the country at top speed. Fogg still had a chance.

They finally stopped at a station by the steamship pier, on the bank of the River Hudson in New York. But the ship to England had already left – only forty-five minutes earlier.

No other steamers could take them across the Atlantic Ocean in time. Passepartout was crushed, but Fogg just visited every ship in the port. Once again, he found a captain who would take passengers.

The ship was sailing to France but that didn't worry Fogg. He simply locked the captain in his cabin and changed course.

The ship was fast but it was now winter and the weather was terrible. Then the engineer gave Fogg more bad news.

"The coal for the boiler is running out!" he said grimly.

"Even my clever master can't solve this," thought Passepartout.

Once again, Fogg surprised him.
He ordered the sailors to cut down
the mast and chop it into logs.

Then he told the astonished men
to burn the wood in the ship's boiler.

Over the next three days, the sailors burned the ship's bridge...

the
cabins...

and even
the decks.

By the time they reached England, only the ship's metal hull was left.

They landed in Liverpool, with just enough time for Fogg to catch a train to London and win his bet. But, as Fogg stepped off the ship, Fix made his move.

"Phileas Fogg," the detective announced, "I arrest you for stealing fifty-five thousand pounds."

Fogg was thrown into prison and there was nothing Princess Aouda or Passepartout could do.

Three hours later, they were waiting for news, when Fix rushed in. His hair was a mess and he looked ashamed. "I've made a dreadful mistake," he cried.

The real thief was arrested three days ago!

Fogg was free again. But he had only five and a half hours left.

Fogg paid for a special train which roared down to London. As it pulled in, he checked the station clock – 8:55. Fogg had lost his bet by just ten minutes.

I don't believe it! We came so close...

Chapter 6

What next?

Phileas Fogg did not show any sign
of how he felt. He simply left the
station with Passepartout and
Aouda and drove home. The next
day, he stayed in his room, adding
up all the money he had lost.

At seven o'clock, Fogg visited Princess Aouda in her room.

"Madam," he said sadly, "When I brought you to England, I planned to give you a fortune. But I am afraid now it is not possible."

"My dear sir," the princess replied gently, "I don't want your money... just you."

Fogg was overjoyed and, for the first time in his life, it showed. "Passepartout!" he called. "Run to the church and book our wedding for tomorrow!"

59

Meanwhile Fogg's friends at his club had spent the last few days in a fever of excitement. They had not heard a word from Fogg since he left on October 2nd.

On the evening of December 21st, they waited eagerly to see if he would show. And, as the hands on the clock reached 8:44, they heard a knock on the door.

Here I am, gentlemen!

It was Phileas Fogg in person.
But how had he done it? Well,
Passepartout had returned from
the priest with incredible news.

"Not Monday tomorrow," he
gasped. "To-tomorrow, Sunday.
Today is... SATURDAY!"

Going around the world to the
east had gained Fogg an extra
day. He'd had ten minutes left to
get to the club and win his bet.

Fogg won twenty thousand pounds but, as he had spent nearly nineteen thousand pounds on the way, he wasn't much better off.

On the other hand, he did find a wife and happiness on his trip. Most people would go around the world for less!

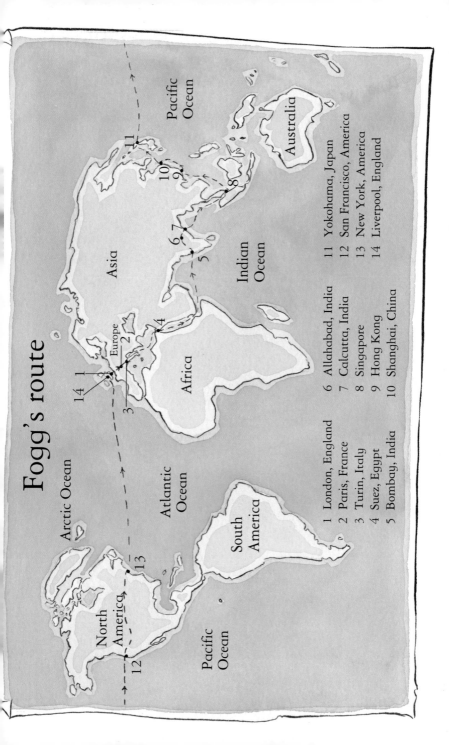

Fogg's route

Arctic Ocean

Pacific Ocean

Europe

Asia

Africa

Atlantic Ocean

North America

South America

Pacific Ocean

Indian Ocean

Australia

1 London, England
2 Paris, France
3 Turin, Italy
4 Suez, Egypt
5 Bombay, India

6 Allahabad, India
7 Calcutta, India
8 Singapore
9 Hong Kong
10 Shanghai, China

11 Yokohama, Japan
12 San Francisco, America
13 New York, America
14 Liverpool, England

Jules Verne (1828-1905) was a French writer who loved science and travel. He combined them with adventure in his stories. His first book, *Five Weeks in a Balloon*, was published in 1863. Ten years later, he wrote *Around the World in Eighty Days*. Another of his famous stories is *Twenty Thousand Leagues Under the Sea*.

Series editor: Lesley Sims

Designed by
Russell Punter

This edition first published in 2004 by Usborne Publishing Ltd.,
Usborne House, 83-85 Saffron Hill, London EC1N 8RT, England.
www.usborne.com
Copyright © 2004 Usborne Publishing Ltd.